# The Treasury of Classic Children's Stories

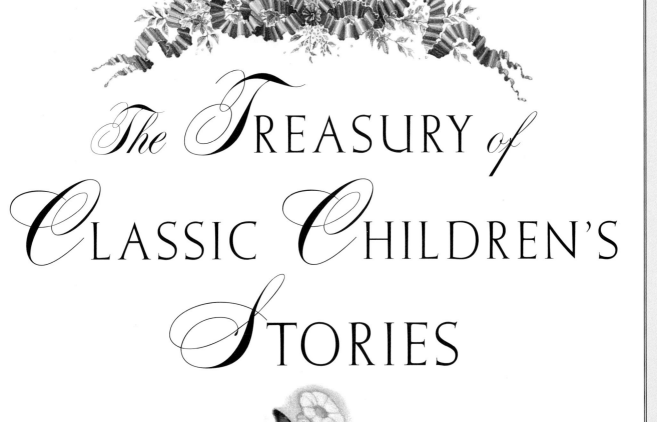

# *The* TREASURY *of* CLASSIC CHILDREN'S STORIES

*Ariel Books*

ANDREWS AND McMEEL
*Kansas City*

Cover painting by Ruth Sanderson

ISBN-13: 978-0-7407-2572-2
ISBN-10: 0-7407-2572-6

# Contents

_The_ TREASURY _of_ CLASSIC CHILDREN'S STORIES

# THE LITTLE MERMAID

By HANS CHRISTIAN ANDERSEN

Retold by JENNIFER GREENWAY

Illustrated by ROBYN OFFICER

$\mathcal{D}$eep in the blue sparkling ocean, deeper than any human has ever gone, the Sea King lived with his subjects in a splendid palace made of rare seashells and pearls.

Now, the Sea King had six beautiful mermaid daughters. The youngest one was the most beautiful. And she was much quieter and more thoughtful than her sisters. While her sisters enjoyed playing with

silvery fish and making wreaths of colored seaweed, the youngest found no amusement in such games. She liked more than anything to hear of the world above the sea, and she often asked her grandmother what it was like.

The little mermaid loved to hear how flowers on land had a fragrance—so different from those under the water, which had none. She was also delighted to learn that the fishes on land—for that's what grandmother called birds—sang beautiful songs. But best of all she liked to hear about the human beings who lived in the world above the waves.

When the daughters of the Sea King reached their fifteenth year, they were allowed to go to the surface of the water. But the little mermaid, being the youngest, watched all her sisters go before her.

When the oldest sister came back, she spoke of the twinkling stars. The second described a beautiful sunset. The third saw a garden full of flowers. The fourth told about the vast blue sky, and the fifth was amazed by giant pale icebergs floating in the ocean. Yet despite the wonderful sights above the water, all the little mermaid's sisters agreed that the world beneath the waves was far more beautiful.

"I shall have to see for myself," the little mermaid thought wistfully. "How I wish my turn would come."

At last, the little mermaid's fifteenth birthday came, and up she went to the world above the waves.

It was evening and the sky sparkled with silver stars. A ship lit with colored lanterns sailed toward the little mermaid. The people on board were having a party. The little mermaid swam up and peered through the window of one of the cabins.

Inside she saw a handsome prince laughing and talking with his friends. He had just turned sixteen years old, and the party was in honor of his birthday.

The little mermaid fell in love with him at once. "If only he could see me," she thought, "perhaps he would love me, too."

Just then the little mermaid saw that a terrible storm was blowing up. The waves began rising higher and higher, and the wind whistled. Soon the ship began to creak and groan. "We're going to sink!" the little mermaid heard one of the sailors yell.

Finally the ship began breaking apart, and
everyone on board was cast into the water. At first,
the little mermaid was glad, since now the handsome
prince would be with her. Then she remembered that
humans could not live underwater.

"I must save him!" the little mermaid thought.
She dove again and again. At last, she found the
prince deep beneath the waves. He was still alive.

She pulled him to the surface. She held his head
above the water, and they drifted all night.

By dawn, the storm had passed and the little mermaid saw a quiet beach. Just beyond the beach, a white church nestled on a hill. She swam to the shore while still holding the prince and dragged him onto the sand. She kissed him on the forehead, but he did not wake up.

Then the church bell rang and a group of young women ran out of the church door. The sound of their voices frightened the little mermaid and she hid behind a rock.

One of the young women ran onto the beach and up to the prince as he was opening his eyes. She was very beautiful, and the prince smiled at her.

"You have saved my life!" he said, for he did not know it was the little mermaid who had really saved him.

Then the young woman helped the prince to his feet and led him away to the white church.

The little mermaid sighed and swam under the waves back to her father's palace. When her sisters asked her what she had seen above the waves, she would not answer. But day and night she thought of the handsome prince, and she grew sad and pale.

The little mermaid began to spend all her time roaming the world above the waves looking for the prince.

One day, she came to a beach where a large marble palace stood. To her joy, she saw the prince walking along the shore, for this palace was his.

After that the little mermaid came every day to secretly watch the prince. Her love for him grew. But she dared not show herself, because her grandmother had told her that humans were afraid of mermaids.

"They believe that everyone should have two of those props they call legs," her grandmother had said. "And they think our tails are very ugly!"

"Ah, if only I had legs," the little mermaid thought. "Perhaps then I could make the prince love me!" Then the little mermaid decided to do a terrible thing.

In the very depths of the ocean, there lived an ancient sea witch. She was wicked but very powerful. So the little mermaid went to seek her advice.

When the little mermaid entered the sea witch's cave, the sea witch stared at her and cackled. "I know why you have come, foolish princess," she said. "I can give you legs, but it will not be easy for you. You will be as graceful as you are now, but each step you take will feel as if you are treading on sharp knives!"

"I do not mind," replied the little mermaid, thinking only of the prince.

"There is more," the sea witch went on. "Once you have taken a human form, you will never be able to live with your family under the waves again. Moreover, if the prince does not love you in return and agree to marry you, you will perish. The morning after he marries another, your heart will break and you will be nothing—only the foam on the waves!"

The little mermaid turned pale. "I will still do it," she said.

"But I must be paid," said the sea witch. "In return for giving you legs I must have your voice."

The little mermaid faltered. Her voice was the loveliest of all the sea creatures, and far more beautiful than that of any mortal. "But how will I make the prince love me without my voice!" she cried.

"You are very lovely," said the witch. "Use that to charm him."

"Very well," said the little mermaid.

So the little mermaid gave her voice to the sea witch, and in return the sea witch gave her the magic potion that would make her legs.

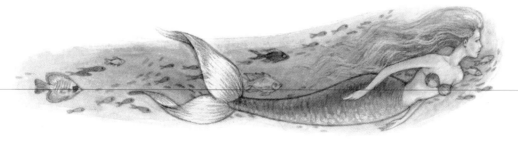

The little mermaid waited
until night and sadly bid farewell to
her sleeping father, grandmother, and
sisters. Then she swam to the beach
near the prince's palace and swallowed
the sea witch's potion.

She felt as if a sword had been passed
through her, and she fainted. When she awoke it was
morning, and to her surprise the prince was standing
over her. The little mermaid looked down and saw
that she had two pretty legs and dainty feet.

"Who are you?" the prince asked, but the little
mermaid could not answer. She was so lovely
and her blue eyes looked so sad that the
prince took pity on her and led her
to his palace.

As the sea witch had promised, every step the little mermaid took was as painful as stepping on sharp knives. But she bore it bravely.

The prince ordered his servants to dress her in fine robes. When this was done, the little mermaid was the most beautiful young woman in the palace. Yet she still could not utter a word, only stare at the prince with her sad, blue eyes.

"You poor creature," the prince said. "If only you could speak to me. You remind me of a girl I met once who saved my life when I almost drowned. She is the only woman I can ever love, but I shall never see her again. So will you stay with me instead?"

When she heard that, the little mermaid's heart almost broke. She wished she could tell the prince that it was she who had saved his life. But she could not say a word.

The prince made the little mermaid his closest companion. She did all she could to please him, but he spoke only of the one who had saved him. "I shall never see her again," he told the little mermaid. "But I am glad that you at least have been sent to me, my beautiful silent friend."

Then the little mermaid danced for him, though it hurt her terribly. She danced so gracefully the prince was enchanted and said she must stay with him always.

One day the king announced that the prince must marry the daughter of the neighboring king. The prince told the little mermaid that he would never do so. "I cannot marry that princess when I love only the girl who saved me," he said. "I would rather marry you than anyone but her." Then he kissed the little mermaid on the cheek.

The next day the king prepared a ship to travel to the nearby kingdom. The little mermaid accompanied the prince on the journey.

When the ship reached the shore, the neighboring king and the princess were there to greet them.

When the prince saw the princess, he cried, "But she is the one who saved my life! All my wishes have come true!" As soon as he was on land, he ran to the princess, leaving the little mermaid standing alone.

The princess was very beautiful and her eyes were kind and gentle. The little mermaid stared at her. "She is lovely and she seems good," the mermaid thought. "The prince loves her, for how can he know that it was I who saved his life and not she? So now I must prepare to die."

The wedding of the prince and the princess was celebrated that very night.

The prince asked the little mermaid to stand close to him during the wedding. "You must share in my happiness," he said. So the little mermaid held up the bride's veil and smiled, even though her heart was broken.

"Tomorrow I must die," she thought. "I will never see my dear sisters or my father or grandmother again!" And a tear rolled down her cheek.

Late that night the prince and his bride went to bed on the ship that was to carry them back to the prince's kingdom. Meanwhile, the little mermaid stood on the deck and gazed at the sea.

Then she saw her sisters swimming toward her. Their beautiful long hair had all been cut off. The eldest one carried a sharp knife in her hand. They were all weeping as they called to the little mermaid, "Dear sister, we gave our hair to the sea witch in exchange for this knife. Before the sun rises, you must kill the prince with it. Then your legs will disappear and your tail will grow back. After that you may come and live with us under the waves again!"

The little mermaid took the knife and went inside the ship to the prince's room. He lay there asleep beside his bride.

When she saw him, tears came to the little mermaid's eyes, and she ran to the deck and flung the knife into the sea. Then as the sun was rising, she threw herself into the water. She waited to die and become like the foam on the waves. But instead she felt herself being lifted high into the air.

"Where am I?" she cried.

"You are with us, the spirits of the air," replied a host of musical voices. "Because of your good deed, little mermaid, you have been made one of us. You will not die. Instead you will travel around the world spreading peace and kindness, and you will live with us forever."

The little mermaid felt full of joy. Looking down, she saw the prince gazing sadly into the water as if he were looking for her. She flew down to him and whispered, "Do not be sad! All is well!"

As the prince's face grew peaceful again, the little mermaid joined hands with the other spirits of the air and rose into the clouds.

# THE FROG PRINCE

By THE BROTHERS GRIMM

Retold by FIONA BLACK

Illustrated by WAYNE PARMENTER

$O$ne sunny day a beautiful princess went for a walk in the woods. After a time, she came upon a cool well and sat down beside it to rest. Then to amuse herself, she began tossing a golden ball in the air and catching it.

This golden ball was the princess's favorite toy, and she often passed her time happily playing this game.

The princess tossed the ball higher and higher in the air. Finally, she tossed it so high that when it came down again, it bounced out of her hands. It rolled away and fell into the well with a loud splash!

The princess sprang to her feet and peered down the well to look for her ball. But the well was very deep—so deep she could not see to the bottom.

The princess began to cry. "How I wish I could get my golden ball back," she sobbed. "I am sure I will never have another one like it!" The more she thought about her ball, the harder she cried, and the harder she cried, the louder her sobs grew.

Suddenly a voice called out to her, "Princess! Why are you crying so?"

The princess lifted her head and looked around to

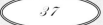

see who was speaking. But all she saw was a large, ugly frog sitting beside the well.

"Princess, please tell me why you are crying!" the frog asked again.

"Oh!" said the princess. She was a little surprised, for she did not know frogs could talk. "It's only you speaking, old frog. It's no good telling you about it, since you can't possibly help me! I've lost my beautiful golden ball down the well, and I am sure I shall never get it back again." With that the princess began to cry even more bitterly than before.

"Please stop crying, princess," said the frog. "I can get your ball back for you. But what will you give me in return?"

"Well," said the princess, drying her tears. "I will give you my fine silk scarf or my pearl necklace or my diamond earrings—or even my ruby and emerald crown! You may have whatever you like, dear frog, only please get me back my golden ball!"

The frog replied that he had no use for the princess's clothes or jewels or anything else that belonged to her.

"I ask only this, dear princess," he said, "that you will let me be your friend and live with you a while. I wish to eat with you from your little golden plate and sleep beside you in your little golden bed. If you promise all this, then I will get your golden ball back for you!"

"How can a frog who swims in a well and croaks all day possibly come and live with me?" the princess thought to herself. "The frog is just being silly! Everyone knows frogs don't eat from plates or sleep in real beds!"

So the princess said to the frog, "I'll promise whatever you like, only please bring back my golden ball!"

At that the frog jumped into the well and swam deep into the cool water. When he came up, he had

the ball in his mouth. He climbed out of the well and dropped the ball at the princess's feet.

"My ball!" she cried happily. Then she picked up the beautiful golden ball and went running off without even saying thank you to the frog.

"Wait! Wait for me!" he croaked, hopping after her. "You promised you would take me with you! I am too small to keep up with you. Wait!"

But the princess did not wait. Instead she ran home and quickly forgot all about the wet, ugly frog.

The next day, as the princess sat down to dinner with the king and the rest of the court, she heard a strange noise outside. Flip-flap, flip-flap, flip-flap it went—as if someone were flopping up the palace steps.

Then there came a soft knocking at the door and a voice implored:

Open the door, princess dear,
Your true friend is waiting here.
Remember what you promised me
By the cool well water deep?

The princess got up and ran to open the door. She was most surprised to see the frog sitting on the doorstep, and she blushed. She slammed the door and ran back to the table and sat down.

The king looked curiously at his daughter.

"You seem flushed," he said to her. "Who was that at the door? A horrible witch or a wicked dragon or a mean giant?"

The princess sighed. "Oh no, father, of course not," she said. "It was only a stupid, nasty frog! You see, I was playing with my golden ball in the woods yesterday when it fell down a deep well. The frog said he'd get the ball back for me if I promised to be his friend and let him live here with me. So I did. Father, I never thought he'd really come. But now here he is!"

No sooner were these words out of the princess's mouth than the frog knocked on the door again.

Then he called out:

Open the door, princess dear,
Your true friend is waiting here.
Remember what you promised me
By the cool well water deep?

The princess clapped her hands over her ears so as
not to hear the frog. The king looked sternly at her

and said, "You gave your promise and now you must keep your word. Go and let the frog in."

The princess made a face. "Yes, father," she said in a small voice. And she went to the door and opened it.

The frog hopped through the door and happily followed the princess to the table. Splish-splash, splish-splash, splish-splash went his green webbed feet. The princess did not like the frog one bit.

She sat down again to eat her dinner, but just as she was lifting her golden fork, the frog called out, "Lift me up beside you. I want to eat, too."

The princess pretended not to hear. Then the king said, "Go on, lift him up! Remember what you promised!"

"Yes, father," said the princess in a very small voice, and she set the frog beside her.

The frog asked her to push her plate closer so he could eat from it, too. The princess did so, but it was plain that she was not happy about it. The frog tasted

everything on her plate and seemed to enjoy the meal very much. But the princess hardly ate anything at all.

When the meal was over the frog said, "Now I am tired. Please take me to your room and let me sleep in your little golden bed!"

The princess scowled. "No! I won't . . . " she began. But then she caught her father's eye and she sighed loudly.

"Very well," she said in a small voice. "Come with me."

Then the princess picked up the wet, nasty frog and climbed slowly up the stairs to her room.

She set the frog down in the corner and climbed into bed. Soon the frog hopped over to her. "I'm tired," he croaked, "and I want to sleep in a comfortable bed just like you!"

The princess put her pillow over her head so she wouldn't have to listen.

"If you don't lift me up onto the bed right now," said the frog, "I'll go and tell your father!"

The princess sighed and pushed aside the pillow. She picked up the frog in her fingers and placed him on her pillow. And there the frog slept all that night.

As soon as the sun rose, the frog woke up. Then he hopped out of the princess's bedroom and down the stairs and through the palace door. He did not come back all day, which was a relief to the princess.

When dinner time came, she looked around anxiously for the frog. But he was nowhere to be seen.

"Thank goodness," thought the princess. "I won't be troubled by that ugly, nasty frog any more!" But that night as the princess was about to go to sleep, there was a knocking at her door. She opened it and there was the frog.

The princess was not pleased. But she picked the frog up and laid him on her pillow without another word. And there he slept all night long.

The next morning the frog left. "Good," thought the princess. "I only hope I never set eyes on that dreadful frog again!" But secretly she did not hate the frog nearly as much as she had at first. Indeed, she almost felt sorry for the creature.

The frog did not appear all that day, nor did he show up at the dinner table. But that night, just as the princess was about to climb into bed, the frog knocked at her door. She picked him up and laid him on her pillow and he fell asleep there.

The next morning when the princess opened her eyes, the frog was nowhere to be seen. Instead, to her astonishment a handsome prince was standing at the foot of her bed and looking at her with a charming smile.

"Who are you?" the princess asked, looking around in bewilderment. "And where is the frog?"

"I am the frog," the prince replied.

The prince then told the princess that a wicked witch had put a spell on him and changed him into an ugly frog. She had sworn that he would remain in this form forever unless a princess took him from the well and let him sleep on her pillow for three nights.

"You have broken the witch's cruel spell," the prince said, "and now I wish to marry you and take you with me to my kingdom. I promise that I will always love you. Marry me and I will do all I can to make you happy."

The princess smiled and gave the prince her hand.

"Very well," she said. "I will marry you, my frog prince."

When the happy couple told the princess's father what had happened, the king was overjoyed and ordered their marriage to be celebrated that very day.

Afterward, the princess and her frog prince set out for his kingdom. As he had promised, the frog prince always loved his princess and treated her kindly. And the two of them lived happily ever after.

# RAPUNZEL

*By* THE BROTHERS GRIMM

*Retold by* FIONA BLACK

*Illustrated by* VICTORIA LISI

There once lived a man and his wife who longed with all their hearts to have a child. At last, their wish was granted, and they were both glad.

Now, this couple's cottage had a window that overlooked a high stone wall. On the other side of the wall was a beautiful garden. This garden belonged to a wicked witch, and no one dared enter it.

One day, as the woman was gazing out the window and down into the garden, she happened to see some rapunzel.

The rapunzel leaves looked so fresh and green that the woman could not help wanting some. "How tasty it would be," she thought, and her mouth began to water. The woman knew she could not possibly have any of the witch's rapunzel, yet her longing for it grew stronger each day. At last, she became so pale and ill, her husband grew worried and asked her what was wrong.

"Ah," sighed the woman. "If I do not get some of the rapunzel from the witch's garden, I will surely die."

The man loved his wife and did not want her to become ill, so he decided he must get her the rapunzel. That night he climbed over the high stone wall and into the witch's garden. He plucked a handful of the rapunzel and quickly returned to his cottage.

The woman prepared a salad of the rapunzel and devoured it at once. But the rapunzel was so delicious that her desire only grew stronger. Her husband became afraid his wife would surely die if she could not have more rapunzel. So that night he once again climbed over the high stone wall and into the witch's garden.

Just as he was about to pick a handful of the rapunzel, he looked up to see the witch standing over him.

"How dare you, you thief!" the witch screamed at him. "Who do you think you are that you may steal rapunzel from my garden? I will make you pay dearly for this!"

The man fell to his knees and begged the witch for mercy. "I only stole the rapunzel for my dear wife," he cried. "I was afraid she would die if she could not have some, and she is about to bear our child."

When the witch heard about the child, she quickly grew calm.

"If what you say is true," she said, "you may take as much of my rapunzel as you like—on one condition! You must give me the child your wife is about to bear. Do not be afraid, I will take good care of your child and love it as a mother would."

Since there was nothing else he could do, the poor man agreed. When his wife gave birth to a girl, the witch took the child away.

The witch named the child Rapunzel and brought her up as her own. Rapunzel grew to be a most beautiful child. Even the blazing sun was in awe of her beauty, as was the shy silvery moon. When Rapunzel was twelve, the witch shut the girl in a high tower in the middle of the forest so no one would ever steal her away.

This tower had no door and no staircase. Instead, there was a single window at the very top. Whenever the witch wanted to visit Rapunzel, she would stand beneath this window and call up:

Rapunzel, Rapunzel,
Let down your hair!

Then Rapunzel, whose golden hair had never been cut, would wind her long, long braid around a hook at the top of the window.

Next she would let it tumble down to the ground like a thick golden rope. Then the witch would climb up it as if it were a ladder, and visit with the girl.

One day a handsome young prince was wandering in the forest near Rapunzel's tower. As the prince rode past the tower, he heard someone singing in a pure, sweet voice. It was Rapunzel, who often passed her lonely days singing to herself.

The prince stopped to listen. The singing was very beautiful, but there was something sad about it, too.

The prince found himself longing to meet the singer. He rode around the tower, looking for a door or a staircase, but he could find no way inside. At last, as it was growing dark, he rode home.

But the prince could not forget Rapunzel's singing. So he returned to the tower the very next day.

The prince was listening to Rapunzel's singing from behind a tree, when the old witch appeared. The prince watched, while she called up to the high window:

Rapunzel, Rapunzel,
Let down your hair!

The prince was amazed to see a braid of thick golden hair tumble out the window. Then he saw how the witch climbed up it into the tower.

"So that is how it is done," the prince said to himself.

As soon as the witch had climbed down and left, the prince ran to the tower. Then he called:

Rapunzel, Rapunzel,
Let down your hair!

Immediately Rapunzel let down her shining golden braid. The prince quickly climbed up it and was soon standing in Rapunzel's tower room.

At first, Rapunzel was very frightened of the prince, for she had never seen a man before. "Who are you?" she cried, backing away.

The prince told Rapunzel his name. Then, speaking to her gently, he said, "Your singing so touched my heart that I could not live in peace until I met you." As he talked, Rapunzel began to lose her fear. Indeed, he was a much more charming companion than the witch.

After that, the prince visited Rapunzel daily—but only in the evening since the witch came during the day. Soon the two young people grew to love each

other. One day the prince asked Rapunzel if she
would marry him.

"Yes," Rapunzel replied. "I will gladly marry you.
But first I must find a way to escape this tower."

Then Rapunzel told the prince that every time
he visited, he must bring her some strong silk thread.
"I will ply it into rope," she said. "And when it is
finished, I will climb down from the tower and we
can be together always."

Every day the prince brought a skein of silk
thread. The witch suspected nothing. Finally, the
rope was almost finished. Then, one day, when the
witch came to see Rapunzel, the girl carelessly said,
"Oh, Granny, why does it take you so much longer to
climb up here than it does the prince?"

"What are you saying, you wicked child?" the
witch snapped.

"Nothing," stammered the girl, realizing what she had done. But it was too late.

"I shut you away from the world, and still you have managed to betray me!" the witch shrieked.

The witch seized Rapunzel's one braid in her right hand and twisted it tight. Then with her left hand she took a pair of scissors and—snip!—she cut off Rapunzel's long golden braid.

Then the witch took the weeping Rapunzel far away to a barren desert. There she left the girl to live in poverty and misery.

That evening the prince came to the tower and called:

Rapunzel, Rapunzel,
Let down your hair!

The long shining hair came cascading down as usual, and the prince climbed up to the window.

Inside the tower he found waiting for him, not his dear Rapunzel, but the wicked witch.

"Your beautiful songbird has flown away!" the witch crooned mockingly. "The cat has got her. And now the cat's going to scratch out your eyes!"

Then she rushed at the prince. In his grief and confusion, he leaped out the window. Some bushes broke his fall and saved his life. But their sharp thorns put out both his eyes.

For several years, the prince wandered blind and almost out of his mind with sorrow. By chance, he came to the desert place where Rapunzel was living.

He heard a pure, lovely, familiar voice singing a sad song. It was Rapunzel, and as the prince drew close, she recognized him. She threw her arms around his neck and began to weep.

When her tears fell into his eyes, his sight became clear again, and the prince saw his dear Rapunzel. He took her to his kingdom where they were married. And they both lived happily together.

# Nutcracker

By E.T.A. HOFFMANN

Retold by FIONA BLACK

Illustrated by SCOTT GUSTAFSON

It was Christmas Eve. The Stahlbaum family was gathered around a tall Christmas tree that was beautifully decorated with glowing candles, candied apples, and sugar almonds. The children, Fritz and Marie, were playing with their new presents when a strange little man with long white hair and a black patch over one eye entered the room.

"Godpapa Drosselmier," the children cried happily as they rushed to him. Despite his odd appearance, their godfather was very kind and clever. He could fix any watch or clock, and he had made them many remarkable toys, too.

"Merry Christmas!" said Godpapa Drosselmier as he handed each child a present. Fritz's gift was a set of tin soldiers, each carrying a handsome sword. Marie's gift was a little wooden man in a bright red uniform.

"Please take good care of this little fellow, Marie," her godfather said solemnly. "He means a great deal to me!"

Marie took the little man in her arms. Despite his elegant uniform and bright paint, he was rather ugly. His head was far too big for his body, and his mouth cut from ear to ear!

"Why, it's a nutcracker!" cried her father. Then
he showed Marie how to put a nut in
the little man's mouth and shut it
tight. There was a quick crack,
and the nutshell fell to the
floor.

Marie hugged the nutcracker.
"Thank you, Godpapa,"
she cried. "He is my favorite
present!"

"How can you like such an ugly
fellow?" said Fritz scornfully.

"Don't say that," cried Marie. "You'll hurt his
feelings!"

"I'm afraid Fritz is right," Godpapa Drosselmier
said. "Our poor nutcracker is rather ugly. If you like,
I'll tell you the story of
how ugliness came into his
family."

"Oh, please do!" begged the children.

"Very well," began their godfather. And this is the tale he told.

Many years ago there lived a king who had a very beautiful daughter. Her name was Princess Pirlipat. She had golden hair and rosy cheeks. Her father adored her and one year he planned a great feast in honor of her birthday.

Now the king was very fond of sausages, and the queen always made them herself. So in honor of the celebration the king asked his wife to make three hundred of her best sausages.

Just as the queen had finished making them, Dame Mouserink, the queen of mice, came into the kitchen. "Let me taste a bit of sausage!" she squeaked.

"Of course," the queen replied. Then Dame Mouserink, followed by all her greedy relations, pounced on the sausages and ate them all up!

When the king learned what had happened he was furious. He announced that whoever rid the kingdom of mice would win the princess's hand in marriage.

Now, one of the king's closest advisors was a clever clockmaker. This clockmaker had a nephew. The boy had been orphaned as a baby and raised by the clockmaker. The nephew was a charming, handsome young man and had the remarkable ability of cracking even the hardest nuts with his teeth. Everyone called him "The Handsome Nutcracker."

The clockmaker decided it would be a fine thing if his nephew married the beautiful Princess Pirlipat. So he began to plan the world's first mousetrap. He baited his traps with sausage. Then he had his nephew set the traps throughout the palace. All of Dame Mouserink's greedy relatives were soon trapped and put to death. But Dame

Mouserink herself was far too clever to become caught in such a way.

Nevertheless, the king was overjoyed and summoned the clockmaker's nephew. With great fanfare he announced that the boy could one day marry the lovely princess.

No sooner had he spoken than Dame Mouserink appeared and made this pronouncement:

I, queen of mice, pronounce this curse:

The Handsome Nutcracker shall become
hideously ugly.
And for him I predict the worst:

My son, the mouse with seven crowns,
Will surely bring the Nutcracker down!

The king's soldiers quickly fell on Dame
Mouserink and killed her. Then Princess Pirlipat
looked at the clockmaker's nephew and shrieked,
"Oh, how ugly he is! I will never marry him!" You
see, the clockmaker's handsome nephew had
changed. He now had a
huge misshapen head.

The clockmaker was heartbroken and felt he was to blame for his nephew's misfortune. So he visited a famous astrologer to learn how the spell might be broken.

"Do not despair," the astrologer reported after studying the boy's stars. "Your nephew is such a fine young man that he will win a kingdom of his own. But unless he defeats Dame Mouserink's son—the Mouse with Seven Crowns—and wins a lady's heart despite his ugliness, he will never return to his proper form."

"And so," finished Godpapa Drosselmier, "now you know how the mousetrap was invented and why nutcrackers are so ugly."

"What was the clever clockmaker's name?" asked Fritz.

His Godpapa smiled strangely. "Drosselmier," he replied. "Just like mine."

By now it had grown late, and Mrs. Stahlbaum told the children it was time to put their new toys away and go to bed.

Fritz quickly put his soldiers in the toy cabinet in the corner of the room and climbed the stairs to his bedroom. But Marie begged to stay up a little while longer. "I want to put my nutcracker to bed properly," she explained.

After everyone else had gone to bed, the sitting room seemed dark and mysterious. Marie stared into the nutcracker's painted blue eyes. They had such a sad expression that she wondered if her Godpapa's story could be true. "Don't worry, dear nutcracker," she whispered. "I will help you if I can!"

Then the room filled with rustling and rattling noises. Startled, Marie looked around. The clock, which had started to strike the hour, whirred to a stop. Then Marie heard a voice say:

Clocks, listen and stop your ticking.
Now the mouse king is awakening.
In the light of the full moon
Comes the hour of the nutcracker's doom!

At that, hundreds of mice began squeezing through all the cracks in the wall and floor.

They organized themselves into troops and
marched in place. Then the floor cracked open and
from the crack rose a horrible creature—a mouse
with seven heads. The seven heads grew from one
huge body, and each was topped by a shining crown.
The seven heads called the mouse army to order, and
they began marching toward the toy cabinet!

Marie was terrified, but then she heard another
voice cry:

Awake! For the hour has come
When we must fight for our kingdom.
Come, toys, and follow me,
The nutcracker calls to
thee!

Then the nutcracker came marching out of the cabinet with his sword drawn. Marie's dolls and Fritz's tin soldiers leaped down from their shelves in the cabinet and followed him. They were joined by the teddy bears, the puppets, and the stuffed cotton clown.

With the nutcracker leading, the toys bravely advanced toward the mouse king's army. Fritz's tin soldiers loaded their cannons with lemon drops and hazelnuts and fired at the mice. But little by little the mice gained the advantage. They bit the puppets and the stuffed cotton clown and knocked over Fritz's tin soldiers. They soon surrounded the nutcracker.

"Prepare to meet your doom!" squealed the mouse king's seven heads as he scurried toward the nutcracker.

Marie's heart was beating so fast she thought she would faint. But she knew she had to do something to save her friend. So she took off her shoe and threw it at the mouse king.

Then everything around her seemed to grow dark and she fell to the floor.

When Marie opened her eyes, all traces of the battle had vanished. The nutcracker stood beside her holding his sword in one hand and the mouse king's seven crowns in the other.

"Dear Miss Stahlbaum," he said, "thanks to your courage I was saved from certain death. Please come with me. I have marvelous things to show you!" Then he helped Marie to her feet and opened the door of the toy cabinet.

To her amazement Marie found that she was small
enough to step inside the toy cabinet. A bright light
washed over her. Then she found herself in a meadow
that glittered with a rainbow of colors. "This is
Candy Meadow," the nutcracker said. "We are in my
kingdom, which is called Toyland."

He led Marie through a gate made of raisins
and almonds and down a road of brightly colored
hard candies. Soon they were in a gingerbread town
where gingerbread men and women waved at them
as they passed.

They came to another town. This one was made of spun sugar and dainty china and glass people sang to them.

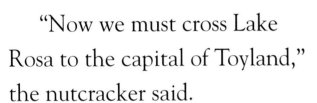

"Now we must cross Lake Rosa to the capital of Toyland," the nutcracker said.

As he spoke, Marie saw a beautiful rose-colored lake and on it there was a little gold boat pulled by dolphins.

She and the nutcracker stepped into the boat and were soon pulled across the lake. Ahead, Marie could see a beautiful city made of sugar plums and candied fruits. But most wonderful of all was a lofty castle with tall rose-colored spires.

"This is my home, Marzipan Castle," said the nutcracker.

Elegantly dressed little dolls greeted them, "Hail to the King of Toyland!" Up until then Marie had been too dazzled by everything she saw to say a word. But now she turned to the nutcracker and cried, "Then Godpapa's story is true, and you are his nephew!"

"Yes," replied the nutcracker. "With your help, I have defeated the mouse king and won back my kingdom, and yet . . . " He sighed so sorrowfully that Marie was sure he must be thinking of the lovely Princess Pirlipat, who had refused his hand.

"I don't understand why the princess was so mean," Marie said, feeling very sorry for the nutcracker. "I would have remained your friend and companion no matter what you looked like. I would not have minded one bit if you were in the shape of a nutcracker!"

As soon as Marie had spoken, a strange thing happened. The castle around her wavered and then disappeared, and Marie felt as if she were falling and falling.

When she landed she was lying in her own bed, and her mother was standing over her. "Wake up, Sleepy Head," Mother said. "It is Christmas morning."

"Oh, Mother," Marie said. "So much has happened!" And she told her mother about the nutcracker and the mouse king and her visit to Toyland.

"You have had a long, beautiful dream," her mother said. "But now you must get up. We have

visitors. Godpapa Drosselmier is here with his nephew."

Marie quickly dressed and ran downstairs. In the sitting room beside the toy cabinet stood her god-papa. Beside him was a handsome young man just her age. His eyes were as blue and kind as those of her own dear nutcracker. Marie knew that she had not been dreaming after all.

Godpapa Drosselmier left the two children alone. Then his nephew knelt before Marie. "Dear Marie Stahlbaum," he said, "by pledging to be my friend despite my ugliness, you have broken Dame Mouserink's curse. Now I beg you to be my friend always and to rule with me over my kingdom."

Marie smiled and said, "Oh, yes!" And when she was grown up, she married young Drosselmier. Then they went to the Marzipan Castle, and today they still rule over the magical Kingdom of Toyland.

# CINDERELLA

*Retold by* SAMANTHA EASTON

*Illustrated by* LYNN BYWATERS

$O$nce upon a time there lived a rich but meek man whose wife had died. After a time, he married again. His second wife was very proud and ill-tempered, and she had two daughters who were just like her.

Now, this man had a daughter from his first marriage. She was very good and beautiful, which made her stepmother and stepsisters jealous.

It wasn't long before the stepmother and her daughters began to treat the poor girl very badly. They made her do the cooking and cleaning, and gave her only an old gray smock to wear. Instead of sleeping in a bed, she had to sleep on the hearth among the cinders. And that was how she came to be called Cinderella.

One day, Cinderella's stepsisters received invitations to a ball that the king was giving for his son. All the young ladies of the kingdom were invited, for the prince wished to choose one of them as his bride.

Cinderella's stepsisters were overjoyed. From that moment on, they could talk of nothing except what they would wear to the ball.

"I shall wear my gold embroidered gown," said the elder. "The prince will surely notice me in that!"

"And I shall wear my red velvet gown," said the younger. "Mother has always told me I look best in red!"

And on and on they talked and planned. They were each determined to be the most beautiful lady at the ball.

At last, the day arrived.

All day Cinderella's stepsisters shouted orders at her. "Cinderella, iron my silk petticoat!" said one. "Curl my hair!" said the other. "Tie this ribbon!" said the first. "Polish my shoes!" said the other. Cinderella didn't complain but did their every bidding.

At last her stepsisters were dressed and ready. As she saw them to the door, Cinderella could not help but sigh, "How I wish I were going to the ball."

Her stepsisters stared at her. "You?" mocked the elder. "What an idea. How could you go to the ball?"

"Besides, whatever would you wear?" said the younger. "Your tattered gray dress with your patched apron?"

Then they both burst into laughter and stepped into their coach.

After her stepsisters had gone, Cinderella sat by the hearth and cried.

Then a voice beside her asked, "Cinderella, why are you crying?"

Cinderella looked up. There stood an old woman wearing a white dress covered with silver stars. In her hand she held a sparkling wand. "I am crying because . . ." she stammered.

"Because you would like to go to the ball," the old woman finished for her. "And so you shall. I am your fairy godmother and I have come here tonight to make all your wishes come true."

Before Cinderella could say another word, her fairy godmother led her into the pumpkin patch in the garden. "First, we must choose a large, round pumpkin," she said. "That one looks about right!"

As Cinderella watched in amazement, her fairy godmother waved her magic wand over the pumpkin and it was transformed into a gold coach!

"Now," said Cinderella's fairy godmother, "let us find the mousetrap and see if there are any mice."

Inside the trap were six gray mice. The fairy godmother waved her magic wand again, and in the twinkling of an eye, they were turned into six fine dappled horses.

"Now, let's look in the rattrap," said the fairy godmother. Inside there was a fat white rat. The fairy godmother touched it with her wand, and instead there stood a jolly coachman with wonderful long whiskers.

"Now, go to the lily pond," Cinderella's fairy god-mother told her. "If you find six green frogs sitting on a log, bring them to me."

And Cinderella did so. With a wave of her magic wand, her fairy godmother turned the frogs into six merry footmen, all dressed in handsome suits of green.

Cinderella was overjoyed. But then she looked down at her old gray smock and her face fell.

"Don't worry!" her fairy godmother said kindly. "I have thought of that, too."

She waved her magic wand once more, and the tattered gray smock became the most beautiful gown Cinderella had ever seen. The dress was made of silver and gold, and was studded with precious gems. Then her fairy godmother brought from her pocket a pair of sparkling glass slippers.

"Now, you are ready to go to the ball," she said with a smile. "But be warned! You must return before the clock strikes twelve. At that hour my magic will fade. Your gold coach will turn back into a pumpkin. Your horses will be mice, your coachman, a rat, and your footmen, only frogs. And your beautiful gown will once again be a tattered gray smock."

Cinderella gave her promise. Then she thanked her fairy godmother and set off happily to the king's palace.

When Cinderella entered the king's great ballroom, she looked so lovely that everyone stopped talking and eating to look at her.

"Who can she be?" they whispered. Her stepsisters, who did not recognize her, said that Cinderella must be a princess from a faraway land. "Who else would be wearing such a splendid gown?" they murmured.

The prince had never seen such a beautiful lady. Immediately, he introduced himself to her and asked her to dance.

Cinderella smiled and nodded. She danced so gracefully that everyone stopped dancing and watched her in admiration.

All night long the prince danced with Cinderella, and Cinderella only. She had never been so happy. She felt as if she were in a beautiful dream.

Cinderella was enjoying herself so much that she did not notice the time passing. Suddenly, the clock began to strike twelve.

"Good-bye!" she called to the startled prince as she dashed from the ballroom. The prince ran after her, but Cinderella was too quick for him.

In her haste, she lost one of her sparkling glass slippers on the palace steps. But there was no time to stop for anything. Just as she reached the gate, the last stroke of midnight rang out. Her beautiful gown turned back into her old gray smock, and her gold coach became a pumpkin. She watched as the mice and the frogs and the rat scurried off. And then she slowly walked home.

The next morning, the prince found Cinderella's glass slipper on the palace steps. It was the most delicate slipper he had ever seen. He carefully picked it up and carried it to his father. "I will marry only the woman whose foot this slipper fits, and no other," he told the king.

At once the king sent his servants throughout the kingdom to try the glass slipper on each lady.

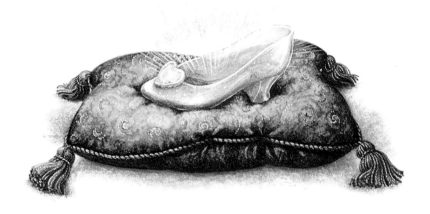

All sorts of young ladies—tall and short, plump and thin, rich and poor—tried on the beautiful glass slipper. But not one of them could get it to fit.

At last, the king's servants came to Cinderella's house. Her two stepsisters were eager to try on the slipper, since they both considered their feet to be small and dainty.

First the elder stepsister tried to get the slipper on, but it would not even go over her toes. She pushed and pulled, but it was no use. Then the younger stepsister tried it on. She tugged and winced, but she could not get the slipper on over her heel.

Then Cinderella said, "May I try, too?"

Her stepsisters rolled their eyes and said, "The slipper will never fit you!"

But the king's servant said that it was only right that she be allowed to try. So Cinderella stretched out her foot.

The stepsisters were surprised. The glass slipper fit Cinderella's foot so perfectly it might just as well have been made for her!

To their further amazement, Cinderella reached into her pocket and brought out the matching glass slipper.

At that moment, Cinderella's fairy godmother appeared, but only Cinderella could see her. With a wave of her magic wand, she turned Cinderella's rags into a gown even more beautiful than the one she had worn to the ball.

Her stepsisters then recognized Cinderella as the lovely princess from the ball. They knelt before her and apologized for treating her so badly. Then Cinderella, who was as kind as she was beautiful, said, "It's all right, sisters. I forgive you both."

The king's servants took Cinderella to the palace to see the prince. He was overjoyed to see her again, and asked her to become his dear wife.

Cinderella and her prince were married that very day. Everyone in the kingdom was invited, even Cinderella's stepmother and stepsisters. It was the most splendid and joyful wedding anyone had ever seen, and Cinderella and her prince lived happily ever after.

# PETER
## and the WOLF

*Retold by* SAMANTHA EASTON

*Illustrated by* RICHARD BERNAL

*L*ong ago in Russia there lived a boy named Peter. Peter lived with his grandfather in a wooden house with a little garden beside it. Surrounding the house and garden was a high stone wall.

On the other side of the wall was a wide green meadow, and beyond that was a great forest. Peter longed more than anything to play in the meadow and explore the forest.

Now Peter's grandfather had told him many times that he was never to go beyond the high stone wall and into the meadow.

"Why not, Grandpapa?" Peter had asked.

"Because," replied his grandfather, "if you go into the meadow a fierce wolf might come out of the forest, and what would you do then?"

Peter didn't answer, but to himself he thought, "If a wolf came out of the forest, I would catch him!"

One morning Peter woke up very early. When he looked outside, he saw the sun rising. A little bird was singing in the birch tree outside his window. The bird was Peter's friend and she chirped to him, "What a beautiful day it is!"

It was a beautiful day, indeed! Peter pulled on his clothes and tiptoed downstairs. Then he raced into the garden.

The little bird flew down and perched on his shoulder. "How nice the meadow looks!" she sang. Peter peered through the gate. The tall green grass was waving in the breeze. The pond in the meadow was blue and sparkling. It was a perfect day to go exploring!

Peter looked over his shoulder at the house. It was dark and quiet. "Grandpapa must still be sleeping!" Peter thought.

Then Peter opened the gate and stepped into the green meadow!

In his haste, Peter neglected to shut the gate, and the duck followed after him.

"I shall have a lovely swim in the pond!" she quacked happily. She waddled to the edge of the pond and slid into the water.

The little bird watched her curiously. Then she flew from Peter's shoulder to the pond.

"Who are you?" she chirped at the duck. "What kind of bird are you if you can't fly?"

"Indeed!" replied the duck crossly. "Well, what kind of bird are you if you can't swim?"

Then the little bird and the duck began to argue. The duck swam in circles around the pond, quacking and ruffling her tail feathers. Meanwhile the little bird hopped up and down on the bank, chattering excitedly.

Peter laughed and laughed until he saw something slinking through the tall green grass. It was the cat!

Closer and closer she came, creeping along on her silent, velvety paws.

"Those silly birds are too busy fighting to see me coming," she thought. "If I am quick and quiet I shall catch the little one for my breakfast!"

Just then Peter shouted to his friend the little bird, "Look out! Look out!"

In the nick of time the little bird saw the cat and flew to the top of a tall tree!

The cat circled the bottom of the tree, staring up at the little bird. "Should I climb up there?" the cat wondered. But then she thought, "By the time I get all the way up, the little bird will have flown away!"

Peter was watching all this very closely when a voice behind him shouted, "Peter! What are you doing out there?"

It was Grandfather. Peter hung his head.

"I told you not to go into the meadow!" Grandfather said, shaking his finger at Peter. "What if a fierce wolf came out of the forest? What would you do then?"

Peter's grandfather led him back into the garden and locked the gate.

"I have to go to town to do some errands," Grandfather said. "So stay here like a good boy."

Then Grandfather went away, leaving Peter alone in the garden. Peter sat down in front of the house and sighed.

"Don't be sad, Peter," sang his friend the little bird.

"But it isn't fair!" said Peter. "If a wolf came I'd catch him. I know I could!"

Just as Peter said that, a big gray wolf came slinking out of the forest!

At the sight of the wolf, the cat meowed and went racing up the tall tree. The little bird hopped to the end of a long branch to get as far away from the cat as possible.

"Help! Help!" quacked the duck, who was still swimming in the pond. She was so afraid that she flapped out of the water and went running toward the house.

"Oh, no!" cried Peter, for the wolf had spotted the duck and was chasing her.

The duck ran as fast as she could, but she wasn't fast enough to get away from fierce gray wolf!

Soon he caught up with her. He opened his jaws wide, then—gulp—he swallowed the duck in a single bite!

After that the wolf trotted over to the tall tree. He prowled around it, staring hungrily at the cat and the little bird.

"Oh, no!" thought Peter. "I must somehow stop that wolf!"

So Peter ran into the house and returned with a length of rope. Slinging the rope over his shoulder, he climbed the high stone wall. One of the branches of the tall tree reached over the wall, and Peter scrambled across it to the tree.

The little bird immediately flew to Peter and perched on his shoulder. The frightened cat scampered to him, too, and climbed into his arms. Now the little bird was very uneasy about the cat being so close!

"Please," Peter said, "won't you both try to be friends?"

So the cat apologized to the bird and promised never to chase him again. The three of them stared down at the wolf. "But what shall we do now?" said the little bird.

"I have a plan!" said Peter. Peter whispered into the little bird's ear.

"Quick! Fly down to the wolf and circle his head. But be careful that he doesn't catch you. The cat and I will take care of the rest!"

So the little bird flew down to the wolf. She flew all around his head, flitting this way and that! The wolf snapped furiously at her—snap! snap! But the little bird was too quick for him, and he couldn't catch her.

Meanwhile Peter made the rope into a lasso, which he gave to the cat. She took it in her mouth, and while Peter looped the loose end around the tree branch, she crept down the tree with it—closer and closer to the wolf.

The wolf was too busy trying to catch the little bird to notice Peter and the cat. Soon the cat was close enough to slip the lasso over the wolf's tail. Then Peter pulled on the rope as hard as he could!

How the wolf struggled to free himself! Every time the wolf jumped, Peter pulled the rope and raised the wolf higher into the air!

Just then some hunters came along. They had been following the wolf's trail, and when they saw him, they began firing their guns.

"Please don't shoot!" cried Peter. "My friends and I have already caught the wolf. Now we would like to take him to the zoo. Will you help us?"

"Certainly," said the hunters, who were very surprised that such a small boy as Peter had managed to catch a wolf.

So they cut the wolf down from the tree, tied his feet to a pole, and set off to town. What a procession it was! Peter was at the head with the little bird perched on his shoulder and the cat strutting beside him. Then came the hunters carrying the wolf. Peter's grandfather met them and joined the procession, too.

"Hrrumph," said Grandfather as he went. "So Peter caught a wolf. But what if the wolf had caught him? What then?"

"See how clever we are?" the cat said to Peter.

"Yes," chirped the bird. "See what Peter and I caught! How clever we are!"

"Don't forget that I helped, too!" sniffed the cat.

And if you listened very carefully, you could hear the duck in the wolf's stomach. As the wolf swung back and forth on the pole, she quacked, "Let me out! Let me out!" Finally one of the hunters slapped the wolf on the back and out she popped, to the joy of Peter and his friends.

Then the duck ruffled her tail feathers and quacked loudly, "Hooray for Peter who caught the wolf!"

"Hooray!" meowed the cat.

"Hooray!" chirped the little bird.

"Hooray!" said the hunters and even Grandfather, too.

"Hooray!" said Peter.

"I knew I could catch a wolf!"

# $\mathcal{G}$OLDILOCKS

## *and the*

# $\mathcal{T}$HREE $\mathcal{B}$EARS

*Retold by* JENNIFER GREENWAY

*Illustrated by* ELIZABETH MILES

$O$nce upon a time there were three bears who lived in a cottage in the woods. There was a great big Papa Bear, a medium-sized Mama Bear, and a little tiny Baby Bear.

One morning the three bears cooked themselves some porridge for breakfast. Then, as the porridge was much too hot to eat, they went for a walk in the woods while it cooled.

No sooner had they gone, than along came a little girl named Goldilocks.

Goldilocks had been playing in the woods and had gotten lost. When she saw the three bears' cottage, her eyes lit up.

"What a pretty little cottage," she said to herself. "I wonder who lives there?"

So Goldilocks went up to the cottage and knocked on the door. She waited quite a long time, but there was no answer.

Goldilocks walked around to the side of the
cottage. She stood on her tiptoes, pressed her face
to the window, and peered in. She could not see
anyone. She stood still and listened carefully, but she
could hear no one. So she hurried back to the front
door, turned the knob, and walked in!

The first thing Goldilocks saw was a table set with three bowls of porridge. There was a great big bowl for Papa Bear, a medium-sized bowl for Mama Bear, and a little tiny bowl for Baby Bear.

Now Goldilocks was very fond of porridge, and her walk had made her hungry. So she took a taste of the porridge in the great big bowl.

But that porridge was much too hot!

"Ouch!" cried Goldilocks, dropping the spoon.

Next Goldilocks took a taste of the porridge in the medium-sized bowl.

But that porridge was much too cold!

"How nasty," said Goldilocks, making a horrible face. Then she took a taste of the porridge in the little tiny bowl.

That porridge was just right!

"Mmmm," said Goldilocks, with a smile. "This porridge is very tasty!" Then she took another spoonful and another and another. And before Goldilocks knew what she was doing, she had eaten Baby Bear's porridge all up!

Then Goldilocks saw three chairs set before the fireplace. There was a great big chair that belonged to Papa Bear, a medium-sized chair that belonged to Mama Bear, and a little tiny chair that belonged to Baby Bear.

Goldilocks climbed into Papa Bear's great big chair.

"Ouch," she cried, jumping down at once. "That chair is much too hard!"

Next Goldilocks climbed into Mama Bear's medium-sized chair.

"Oh," she cried, as she sank down into the cushions. "This chair is much too soft!"

Then Goldilocks climbed into Baby Bear's little tiny chair.

"Ah," she said, and she smiled and leaned back. "This chair is just right!"

But just as Goldilocks was beginning to feel comfortable, down she tumbled with a crash!

"Oh dear," cried Goldilocks, for Baby Bear's little tiny chair was broken into a thousand pieces!

Next Goldilocks climbed the stairs to the three bears' bedroom. There she saw three beds all in a row. There was a great big bed for Papa Bear, a medium-sized bed for Mama Bear, and a little tiny bed for Baby Bear.

First, Goldilocks climbed into Papa Bear's great big bed and pulled down the covers.

But she jumped down right away.

"Oh no," Goldilocks said. "That bed is much too hard!"

Then she climbed into Mama Bear's medium-sized bed. "Oh dear," said Goldilocks, wrinkling her nose. "This bed is much too soft!"

Then Goldilocks went to Baby Bear's little tiny bed, pulled down the covers, and climbed in.

That bed was just right!

Goldilocks closed her eyes, and soon she was fast asleep.

Then the three bears returned from their walk. They were very hungry and were looking forward to a breakfast of delicious porridge.

As soon as they came inside, the three bears washed their hands and sat down at the table.

Papa Bear stared down at his great big bowl. Then he said in his great big voice, "Someone has been eating my porridge!"

Mama Bear looked down at her bowl. "Oh dear," she said in her medium-sized voice, "someone has been eating my porridge!"

Then Baby Bear looked down at his little tiny bowl. "Someone has been eating my porridge," he cried in his little tiny voice, "and they've eaten it all up!"

Then the three bears walked to their three chairs that were set before the fireplace.

Just as Papa Bear was about to sit down in his great big chair, he growled in his great big voice, "Someone has been sitting in my chair!"

And just as Mama Bear was about to sit down in her medium-sized chair, she cried out in her medium-sized voice, "Someone has been sitting in my chair!"

Baby Bear looked down at his little tiny chair. "Someone has been sitting in my chair," he cried in his little tiny voice, "and they've broken it into a thousand pieces!"

Next the three bears went upstairs to the bedroom.

Papa Bear looked at his great big bed and saw that the covers had been pulled down. Then he frowned and growled in his great big voice, "Someone has been sleeping in my bed!"

Then Mama Bear looked at her medium-sized bed and saw that the pillows had been scattered about.

"And someone has been sleeping in my bed," Mama Bear cried in her medium-sized voice.

Baby Bear looked at his little tiny bed. "And someone has been sleeping in my bed!" he cried in his little tiny voice, "AND HERE SHE IS!"

When Goldilocks heard Baby Bear's little tiny voice, she awoke with a start. She looked up and saw the three bears standing around her.

Goldilocks was so frightened that she leaped out of bed, raced down the stairs, and dashed out the door of the three bears' cottage. And she didn't stop running until she was all the way home.

Then the three bears fixed themselves another breakfast of hot porridge. And they never saw Goldilocks again!

# THE EMPEROR'S NEW CLOTHES

By HANS CHRISTIAN ANDERSEN

Retold by SAMANTHA EASTON

Illustrated by RICHARD WALZ

There was once an emperor who loved new clothes. He spent all his money on clothes and had a different suit for every hour of the day. Unlike other emperors, he cared nothing for his soldiers or his fortresses. Nor did he enjoy going to the theater or reading books. No, the emperor loved clothes more than anything else and was always busy adding to his wardrobe.

The emperor lived in a bustling city with a huge marketplace. Visitors came there from all over the world, so it is not surprising that one day two swindlers also arrived.

When these swindlers learned how fond the emperor was of new clothes, they let it be known that they were famous weavers and that the cloth they made was the finest in the world. Not only were the colors and patterns remarkably beautiful, but the cloth possessed a magical quality. Clothes made from it were completely invisible to anyone who was a fool or unfit for his or her job.

Soon everyone in the city was talking about the marvelous cloth, and of course the emperor came to hear about it, too.

"A suit made of such cloth would be a wonderful thing to have!" the emperor thought. "With a suit like that I would be able to tell at once who was clever and who was stupid and whether the people in my court were really fit for their jobs. I must order a suit of this cloth at once!"

So the emperor summoned the two swindlers to his palace. Then he gave them a large bag of gold so that they would begin work right away.

The swindlers set up their looms in a room in the palace. They ordered the finest silk in all the colors of the rainbow and thread of silver and gold. But they did not use any of this. Instead, they hid it all away. Then they pretended to be hard at work on their empty looms.

After a time the emperor wondered how the marvelous cloth was coming along. He was about to go see for himself, when he remembered that the cloth would be invisible to anyone who was a fool or unfit for his or her office.

Now, the emperor was quite sure he himself had nothing to worry about. Nevertheless, he thought it might be wise to send someone else to look at the cloth first. "I shall send my honest old minister to look at it," the emperor thought. "He's very clever, and he knows his job better than anyone!"

So the honest old minister went to the room where the swindlers were working.

The minister entered the room and was startled to see the swindlers bent over empty looms. "Goodness gracious!" he thought. "I can't see anything at all!" He rubbed his eyes and opened them as wide as possible.

But it did no good. He could not see even a thread of the marvelous cloth.

"Oh, no!" the honest old minister thought. "I never would have believed it. Can it be that I'm a fool or unfit for my position?"

The thought of it was so dreadful that the old minister decided not to say a word about his experience to anyone.

"Do tell us what you think of our lovely cloth," said the swindlers as they bent over their looms.

"It . . . it is very beautiful, indeed," stammered the minister. "What fine colors! What an exquisite pattern! I've never seen anything like it!"

"We thought you would be impressed," said the swindlers. They described the colors and unusual pattern in great detail. The minister listened very carefully so that he would be able to repeat every word to the emperor. Then he went and told the emperor that the cloth was truly marvelous—the finest he had ever seen.

The emperor was delighted. He sent the swindlers another bag of gold and more fine silk and gold and silver thread. As before, the swindlers hid this all away. Then they pretended to work harder than ever on the empty looms.

A while later, the emperor again wondered how the marvelous cloth was coming.

This time the emperor decided to send his most trusted courtier to have a look at it.

Like the old minister before him, the courtier looked and looked and rubbed his eyes and looked again. But no matter what he did, he could see nothing at all.

"Don't you find the cloth exquisite?" asked the swindlers. "Have you ever seen such colors or such a pattern before?"

"How can this be?" the courtier thought. "I know I am not stupid. Can I be unfit for my position? How terrible! I must not let anyone know of this!"

So the courtier praised the cloth highly. "Never have I seen anything to compare with it!" he said. And that was exactly what he told the emperor.

Now, everyone in the city could speak of nothing but the marvelous cloth. So the emperor decided to go see it for himself.

The emperor, followed by all his courtiers and ministers, went to the swindlers' room. When the emperor walked in, the swindlers appeared to be hard at work over the empty looms.

"Isn't the cloth breathtaking!" said the honest old minister. "Has your majesty ever seen such a delicate and unusual pattern?" On and on he went, imagining that all the others could see the beautiful cloth.

The emperor blinked and rubbed his eyes. But he could see nothing at all! "Oh, dear," he thought. "Can I be a fool? Am I unfit to be emperor? This is the worst thing that has ever happened to me! No one must ever suspect!"

Then he said to the swindlers, "I couldn't be more delighted. The cloth is absolutely . . . magnificent!"

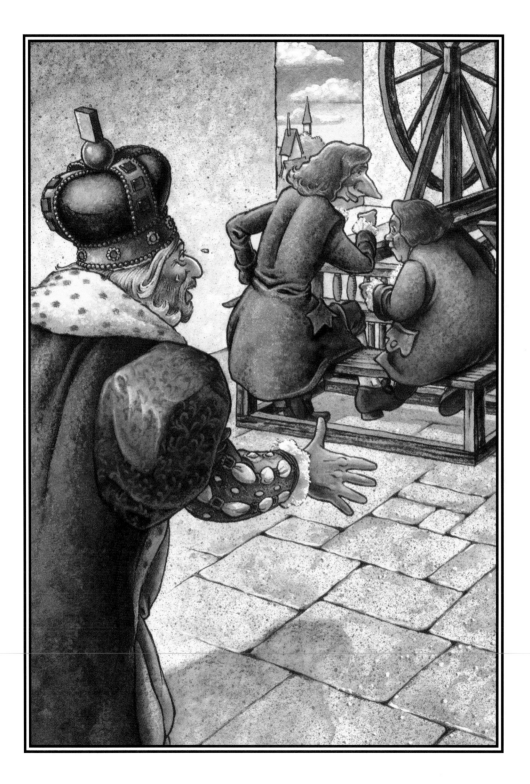

"Stupendously beautiful!" chimed his courtiers. "Excellent in every way," said his ministers. Then they advised the emperor to order a suit of the cloth to be ready to wear in the great procession planned for that very week.

So the emperor did. He gave the swindlers even more gold and appointed them Royal Weavers to the Empire.

On the day before the procession, the two swindlers appeared to be working frantically to finish the emperor's new suit.

All day long they cut through the air with scissors and sewed with needles that had no thread. Everyone

noticed that the candles in their workroom burned all night long. At last, when morning came, the swindlers announced, "The emperor's suit is now finished!"

The emperor, followed by the entire court, proceeded to the swindlers' room.

The swindlers bowed when the emperor entered. Then they held up their empty hands. "Look," they said. "Here is the emperor's new jacket." And "Here

is the emperor's new vest." And "Here are the
emperor's new trousers."

All the courtiers and ministers nodded their heads
in wonder. "What a beautiful suit," they all said.
"Truly splendid!"

The emperor nodded, too. "Yes, indeed," he said.
"I couldn't be more pleased."

"And see how cleverly the suit is made," the
swindlers said. "Feel this jacket. It is as light as air!"

"Why, yes, so it is," said the emperor.

"Now," said the swindlers, "will your majesty be so kind as to undress please, so that your majesty may put on your new suit of clothes?"

They led the emperor to a large mirror. Then they helped him take off his clothes and pretended to put on his new suit piece by piece—first the trousers, then the shirt, then the vest, and then the jacket.

"There!" they exclaimed when they were done. "Doesn't the new suit fit your majesty to perfection?"

The emperor stared at himself in the mirror. He could not see a thing, but he dared not admit it.

"Ah, yes," he said, admiring his reflection. "It looks very nice. Doesn't my new suit become me?" he asked his courtiers and ministers.

"Oh, yes," they agreed. "Your majesty has never looked so splendid in any other clothes."

"And does the pattern really suit me?" asked the emperor, feeling a little uneasy.

"No other pattern could possibly suit you so well!" said his courtiers.

"Very true," said his ministers.

Then the servants who were to carry the emperor's train stepped forward. As they could not see the cloth, they pretended to hold

the train in their hands, and the procession began.

The emperor marched under his splendid velvet canopy, and his servants and footman marched after him. He marched out of the palace gates and through the city streets.

The streets were lined with people, for everyone wanted to see the emperor's new clothes.

As the emperor passed, everyone cried, "Look how splendid the emperor's new suit is! Such colors! Such a pattern!"

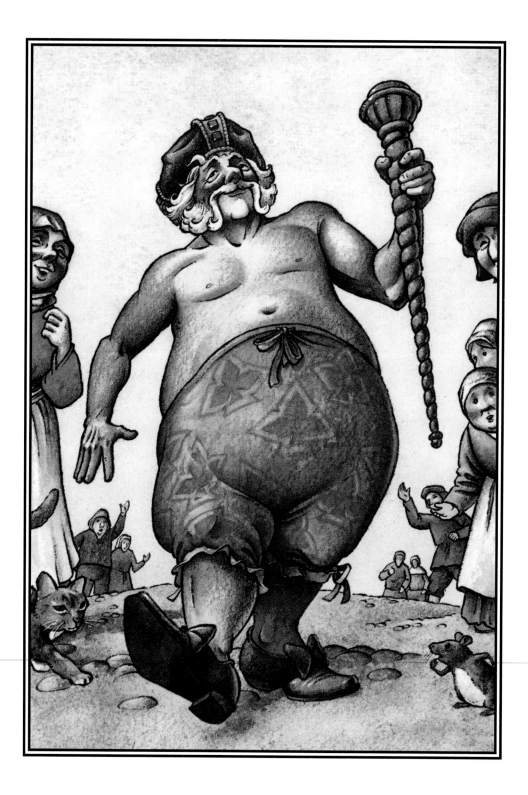

Not a one of them dared let their neighbors know that he could see nothing. They might be thought fools or unfit for their jobs, and that would be dreadful!

So they all praised the emperor's new clothes as loudly as they could. Never had any of the emperor's clothes caused such a stir. Then a small child cried out, "But, Mother, the emperor has nothing on!"

"Shhh," said the child's mother. But then she looked again at the emperor, and said, "Why, it's true. The emperor has nothing on!"

One of her neighbors overheard her, and began shouting it, too. Then all the people shouted at once, "But the emperor has nothing on!"

The emperor could not help hearing them. He blushed bright red, for he realized it was true. But what could he do? So he stood up even straighter and kept walking, wearing only his crown and underclothes. Meanwhile the emperor's servants marched behind him, holding his imaginary train as if nothing were wrong. And so ends the story of the emperor's new clothes!

# Hansel and Gretel

By THE BROTHERS GRIMM

Retold by FIONA BLACK

Illustrated by JOHN GURNEY

In a small cottage at the edge of a large
forest, there once lived a poor woodcutter with his
second wife. Now this woodcutter had two children
from his first marriage, a boy named Hansel and a
girl named Gretel.

Little by little, the woodcutter became poorer and
poorer, until finally he did not have even enough
money for food.

One night, the woodcutter said to his wife, "What are we to do? We cannot feed our children or ourselves."

"There is only one thing to do," his wife replied. "We will give each of the children one last piece of bread. Then we must take them into the forest and leave them there. They can find their own food."

"I cannot do that to my own children!" the woodcutter cried. "They will die in the woods." But his wife nagged him until he agreed with her plan.

Hansel and Gretel were awake and they over-heard their stepmother's words. Gretel began to cry. "Don't be afraid," her brother said. "I am sure I can think of a way to save us."

After his parents were asleep, Hansel crept out of the house. In the garden, the moon shone brightly on the white pebbles, making them gleam like silver.

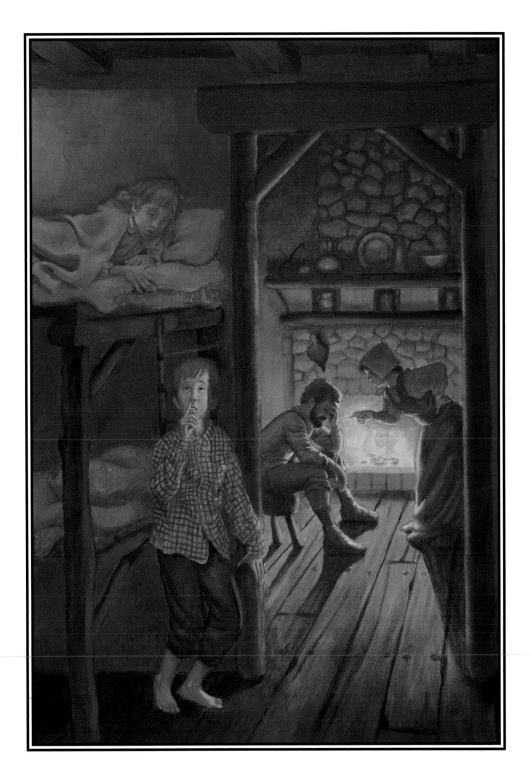

Hansel filled his pockets with pebbles and went back inside. "Sleep in peace, dear Gretel," he said. "All will be well."

Early the next morning, their stepmother shook them awake. "Get up! We are going into the forest to chop wood," she said. "Here is a piece of bread for your lunch. But don't eat it until then, for it's all you'll get!"

Gretel hid Hansel's piece of bread in her apron pocket, as Hansel's pockets were full of pebbles. Then they all started out into the forest.

Along the way Hansel kept turning and looking back at the cottage. "Come along," his father scolded. "Why are you dallying?"

"Oh," Hansel replied. "I am only saying good-bye to my white kitten who is sitting on the roof."

"Don't be silly!" said his stepmother. "That is not your kitten. That's only the sun shining on the roof."

But Hansel was not really saying good-bye to his kitten. Each time he turned he dropped a white pebble on the path.

When they reached the middle of the forest, Hansel's father and stepmother made a big fire. "Stay here by the warm fire and eat your lunch, children," their stepmother said. "Your father and I are going further into the forest to chop wood."

So Hansel and Gretel sat by the fire and ate their bread. They believed their parents were close by, for they thought they heard the chopping of their father's axe. But it was only the wind knocking a dead branch against a tree.

After a while, the children fell asleep. When they awoke, it was dark and their parents were nowhere to be seen. Gretel began to sob, but Hansel said, "Do not fret, little sister. Wait until the moon rises."

And when the moon rose, Hansel took Gretel's hand and they followed the trail of white pebbles home.

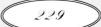

Their father threw his arms around his children, for he was sorry for having left them in the forest. But soon the family was hungry again. One night, Hansel and Gretel heard their stepmother say to their father, "We must get rid of the children! This time we must take them so far into the forest that they will never find their way back!"

When his parents were asleep, Hansel tried to go outside to pick up pebbles. But this time the door was locked.

The next morning, Hansel and Gretel's step-mother gave them each a tiny piece of bread. Then they all set out into the forest.

On the way, Hansel crumbled the bread in his pocket and scattered the crumbs along the path. When his father asked him why he was going so slowly, Hansel replied, "I am only saying good-bye to my pigeon who is cooing on the chimney."

"Don't be silly," his stepmother scolded. "That's not your pigeon. That is only the sun shining on the chimney!"

But Hansel was not really saying good-bye to his pigeon. He was carefully sprinkling crumbs on the path, until all his bread was gone.

This time their parents took Hansel and Gretel to a part of the forest they had never seen before. Then the woodcutter made an even bigger fire. "Eat your bread by the warm fire," their stepmother said. "We are going to chop wood, and we will return for you when we are finished."

Gretel shared her piece of bread with her brother. Then the two children grew drowsy and fell asleep.

When they awoke it was night. They called as loudly as they could for their father and stepmother, but no one came. Gretel began to cry, but Hansel said to her, "Wait until the moon rises. Then we will follow the bread crumbs I scattered all the way home."

But when the moon rose, there were no bread crumbs to be found. The birds of the forest had eaten them all.

"Let us just walk," Hansel said to Gretel. "We will find our way home, you'll see." But they walked all night long and could not find their way out of the forest.

The next day the children walked from dawn to dusk, and still they were lost in the great forest. Nothing they saw looked familiar.

Hansel and Gretel were very hungry, for since finishing their bread, they had eaten nothing except the few nuts they found on the ground. By nightfall, they were too tired and weak to go on any further. They lay down at the foot of a tree and fell asleep.

As soon as Hansel and Gretel awoke the next morning, they began walking. Their hearts were heavy, for they knew that if they did not find a way out of the forest soon, they would surely die there.

Then Hansel and Gretel spotted a beautiful white bird perched on a low branch of a nearby tree. The bird began to sing. Its voice was so sweet that the children stopped to listen. Then the bird flapped its wings and came to fly just ahead of them.

"It is almost as if it were trying to lead us some-where!" Hansel cried.

The children followed the beautiful white bird through the forest, until it brought them to a little house and alighted on its roof.

When Hansel and Gretel drew closer, they saw that the house was made of gingerbread, with a roof of raisin cake. The windows were made of sugar candy, and the eaves and sills were trimmed with sugar icing.

Hansel turned to his sister and said, "Now we shall have a good meal! I'll eat the roof and you start on the windows!"

Hansel broke off a corner of the roof, while Gretel knocked out a windowpane. But just as they began eating, a gruff voice from inside the house cried:

Crunching and nibbling like a mouse!
Who is eating up my house?

Hansel and Gretel replied:

It is just the wind on high,
Blowing, bumping through the sky!

The children were so hungry they could not stop eating. Hansel tore another piece from the roof. Meanwhile, Gretel pulled off a windowsill and gobbled it down.

Just then the door of the gingerbread house flew open, and out hobbled an old woman with a cane.

Hansel and Gretel were frightened, but the old woman said to them kindly, "Don't be afraid. I won't hurt you. Come in!"

The old woman fed them apple pancakes with sugar and raisins. Then she led them to two snug little beds. Hansel and Gretel fell fast asleep, believing they were safe at last.

But the old woman was not as kind as she seemed. She was really a wicked witch who invited children into her gingerbread house so that she could eat them.

Early the next morning the wicked witch shook Hansel awake. She took him to a dark cell beneath the house and locked him inside.

Then the witch went back upstairs to wake Gretel. "Get up," she cackled. "There is work to do! You must cook food for your brother. I wish to make him nice and fat and then I will eat him up!"

Gretel began to weep, but there was nothing she could do.

Every day Hansel was given plenty of good food—chicken and dumplings, thick stews and biscuits, and rich cakes of all kinds. Poor Gretel was fed only dry crusts of bread.

Every day the witch went to Hansel's cell to see how fat he had become. "Stick out your finger," she said, "and let me see if you are plump yet."

Instead of his finger, clever Hansel stuck out a chicken bone. The witch, who was very nearsighted, would feel the bone and go away grumbling because Hansel was still not fat enough to eat.

The old witch grew impatient. One day she decided not to wait anymore and she began to prepare Hansel for eating.

She called Gretel and said, "I wish to bake some bread. I have made the dough and lit the oven. Just crawl inside and tell me if it is hot enough yet."

The witch meant to close the oven door as soon as Gretel was inside and cook her, too. But Gretel knew what the witch was thinking and asked, "How do I get in?"

"How stupid you are!" replied the witch. "Just crawl in. Watch how I do it." And she stuck her head in the oven.

Quickly Gretel shoved the witch into the oven. Then she shut the door and bolted it.

How the witch screamed! But Gretel paid no attention. She ran and unlocked the door to her brother's cell. "Oh, Hansel!" she cried. "The wicked witch is dead and we can leave this place!" She threw her arms around her brother and they both wept with joy.

Now that the witch was dead, Hansel and Gretel decided to explore the gingerbread house. To their delight, they found chests full of gold and jewels. Hansel stuffed his pockets with the riches, and Gretel filled her apron.

Then the two children walked into the forest. They walked all day. Toward evening, they reached the edge of the forest. They came upon a familiar path with flowers growing along it. "Look, Gretel," cried Hansel. "We're not lost anymore!"

In the distance, the children spotted their father's cottage. They began running toward it. When they burst through the door they found their father sitting alone by the fireplace.

The woodcutter was overjoyed to see his children
again. His wife had died, and he had not smiled
once since he had left Hansel and Gretel alone in
the forest.

The children showed him the gold and jewels they
had found in the witch's house. Now, they would all
live happily ever after, and never be hungry again.

# Classic Poems

## for

## Children

Edited by ARMAND EISEN

Illustrated by DEBBIE DIENEMAN

# THE LITTLE LAND

When at home alone I sit
And am very tired of it,
I have just to shut my eyes
To go sailing through the skies—
To go sailing far away
To the pleasant Land of Play;

To the fairy land afar
Where the Little People are;
Where the clover-tops are trees,
And the rain-pools are the seas,
And the leaves like little ships
Sail about on tiny trips.

—ROBERT LOUIS STEVENSON

## THERE WAS AN OLD MAN

There was an Old Man with a beard,
Who said, "It is just as I feared!—
Two Owls and a Hen, four Larks and a Wren,
Have all built their nests in my beard!"

—EDWARD LEAR

## THE OWL

There was an old owl who lived in an oak;
The more he heard, the less he spoke.
The less he spoke, the more he heard.
Why aren't we like that wise old bird?

—ANONYMOUS

## DID YOU EVER GO FISHING?

———❦———

Did you ever go fishing on a bright sunny day—
Sit on a fence and have the fence give way?
Slide off the fence and rip your pants,
And see the little fishes
    do the hootchy-kootchy dance?

—ANONYMOUS

## DUCKS' DITTY

All along the backwater,
Through the rushes tall,
Ducks are a-dabbling,
Up tails all!
Ducks' tails, drakes' tails,
Yellow feet a-quiver,
Yellow bills all out of sight
Busy in the river!

—KENNETH GRAHAME

## THE COW

The friendly cow all red and white,
I love with all my heart:
She gives me cream with all her might,
To eat with apple-tart.

—ROBERT LOUIS STEVENSON

# IF YOU SEE A FAIRY RING

If you see a fairy ring
    In a field of grass,
Very lightly step around,
    Tiptoe as you pass;
Last night fairies frolicked there,
    And they're sleeping somewhere near.

If you see a tiny fairy
    Lying fast asleep,
Shut your eyes and run away,
    Do not stay to peep;
And be sure you never tell,
    Or you'll break a fairy spell.

—ANONYMOUS

## TIME TO RISE

A birdie with a yellow bill
Hopped upon the window-sill,
Cocked his shining eye and said:
"Ain't you 'shamed, you sleepy-head?"

—ROBERT LOUIS STEVENSON

## NOW THE DAY IS OVER

Now the day is over,
Night is drawing nigh,
Shadows of the evening
Steal across the sky.

Now the darkness gathers,
Stars begin to peep,
Birds and beasts and flowers
Soon will be asleep.

—SABINE BARING-GOULD

## MY SHADOW

I have a little shadow
    that goes in and out with me,
And what can be the use of him
    is more than I can see.
He is very, very like me
    from the heels up to the head;
And I see him jump before me,
    when I jump into my bed.

—ROBERT LOUIS STEVENSON

## TWINKLE, TWINKLE, LITTLE STAR

Twinkle, twinkle, little star,
How I wonder what you are!
Up above the world so high,
Like a diamond in the sky.
Twinkle, twinkle, little star,
How I wonder what you are!

—ANONYMOUS

## I SEE THE MOON

I see the moon,
And the moon sees me;
God bless the moon,
And God bless me.

—ANONYMOUS

## A CHILD'S THOUGHT

At seven, when I go to bed,
I find such pictures in my head:
Castles with dragons prowling round,
Gardens where magic fruits are found;
Fair ladies prisoned in a tower,
Or lost in an enchanted bower;
While gallant horsemen ride by streams
That border all this land of dreams
I find, so clearly in my head
At seven, when I go to bed.

—ROBERT LOUIS STEVENSON

## THE LITTLE MOON

The night is come, but not too soon,
And sinking silently,
All silently, the little moon
Drops down behind the sky.

—HENRY WADSWORTH LONGFELLOW

## THE FIREFLY
## LIGHTS HIS LAMP

Although the night is damp,
The little firefly ventures out,
And slowly lights his lamp.

—ANONYMOUS

# WHAT IS PINK?

What is pink? A rose is pink
   By the fountain's brink.
What is red? A poppy's red
   In its barley bed.
What is blue? The sky is blue
   Where the clouds float through.
What is white? A swan is white
   Sailing in the light.
What is yellow? Pears are yellow,
   Rich and ripe and mellow.
What is green? The grass is green,
   With small flowers between.
What is violet? Clouds are violet
   In the summer twilight.
What is orange? Why, an orange,
   Just an orange!

—CHRISTINA ROSSETTI

## PIPPA'S SONG

The year's at the spring,
And day's at the morn;
Morning's at seven;
The hill-side's dew-pearl'd;
The lark's on the wing;
The snail's on the thorn;
God's in His heaven—
All's right with the world!

—ROBERT BROWNING

## FOUR SEASONS

Spring is showery, flowery, bowery.
Summer: hoppy, choppy, poppy.
Autumn: wheezy, sneezy, freezy.
Winter: slippy, drippy, nippy.

—ANONYMOUS

## CATERPILLAR

Brown and furry
Caterpillar in a hurry,
Take your walk
To the shady leaf, or stalk,
Or what not,
Which may be the chosen spot.
No toad spy you,
Hovering bird of prey pass by you;
Spin and die,
To live again a butterfly.

—CHRISTINA ROSSETTI

## WHO HAS SEEN THE WIND?

Who has seen the wind?
Neither I nor you:
But when the leaves hang trembling,
The wind is passing through.

Who has seen the wind?
Neither you nor I:
But when the leaves bow down their heads,
The wind is passing by.

—CHRISTINA ROSSETTI

## THE WIND

I saw you toss the kites on high
And blow the birds about the sky;
And all around I heard you pass,
Like ladies' skirts across the grass—
O wind, a-blowing all day long,
O wind, that sings so loud a song!

—ROBERT LOUIS STEVENSON

## RAIN

The rain is raining all around,
It falls on field and tree,
It rains on the umbrellas here,
And on the ships at sea.

—ROBERT LOUIS STEVENSON

## WHITE CORAL BELLS

White coral bells upon
    a slender stalk.
Lilies of the valley
    deck my garden walk.
O don't you wish that you
    could hear them ring?
That can happen only
    when the fairies sing.

—ANONYMOUS

## THE RAINBOW

There are bridges on the rivers,
As pretty as you please;
But the bow that bridges heaven,
And overtops the trees,
And builds a road from earth to sky,
Is prettier far than these.

—CHRISTINA ROSSETTI

## Sweet and Low

Sweet and low, sweet and low,
    Wind of the western sea,
Low, low, breathe and blow,
    Wind of the western sea!

Over the rolling waters go,
Come from the dying moon, and blow,
    Blow him again to me;
While my little one,
    while my pretty one, sleeps.

—ALFRED, LORD TENNYSON

## THE SEA

Behold the wonders of the mighty deep,
Where crabs and lobsters learn to creep,
And little fishes learn to swim,
And clumsy sailors tumble in.

—ANONYMOUS

## AT THE SEA-SIDE

When I was down beside the sea
A wooden spade they gave to me
To dig the sandy shore.

My holes were empty like a cup.
In every hole the sea came up,
Till it could come no more.

—ROBERT LOUIS STEVENSON

## HAPPY THOUGHT

The world is so full of a number of things,
I'm sure we should all be as happy as kings.

—ROBERT LOUIS STEVENSON

## THE SWING

How do you like to go up in a swing,
Up in the air so blue?
Oh, I do think it the pleasantest thing
Ever a child can do!

—ROBERT LOUIS STEVENSON

## GRASSHOPPERS THREE

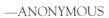

Grasshoppers three a-fiddling went,
Hey, ho, never be still!
They paid no money toward their rent,
But all day long with elbow bent
They fiddled a tune called Rillaby-rill,
Fiddled a tune called Rillaby-ree.

—ANONYMOUS

## THREE GHOSTESSES

Three little ghostesses,
Sitting on postesses,
Eating buttered toastesses,
Greasing their fistesses,
Up to their wristesses,
Oh, what beastesses
To make such feastesses!

—ANONYMOUS

## A WEE LITTLE WORM

A wee little worm in a hickory-nut
Sang, happy as he could be,
"O I live in the heart
    of the whole round world,
And it all belongs to me!"

—JAMES WHITCOMB RILEY

## HURT NO LIVING THING

Hurt no living thing;
Ladybird, nor butterfly,
Nor moth with dusty wing,
Nor cricket chirping cheerily,
Nor grasshopper so light of leap,
Nor dancing gnat, nor beetle fat,
Nor harmless worms that creep.

—CHRISTINA ROSSETTI

# Snow White

*By* THE BROTHERS GRIMM

*Retold by* JENNIFER GREENWAY

*Illustrated by* ERIN AUGENSTINE

*O*ne snowy winter day, a queen sat at the
window sewing on a frame made of ebony. She pricked
her finger with the needle, and three drops of blood
fell in the snow on the windowsill.

The red blood looked so beautiful against the
white snow that the queen exclaimed, "I wish I had a
daughter as white as snow, red as blood, and black as
ebony."

A short time later the queen gave birth to a daughter whose skin was as white as snow, whose cheeks were as red as blood, and whose hair was black as ebony. She named her child Snow White and not long after, the queen died.

Snow White grew up to be the most beautiful girl in the world. She was so good and kind that everyone who met her could not help but love her. Even the birds in the trees and the animals of the woods adored her.

When Snow White was still a child, her father took a second wife. She was a very beautiful woman, but proud and spiteful. She could not bear the thought that anyone else might be as beautiful as she.

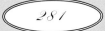

Now this queen had a magic mirror and whenever she looked into it, she would say:

Mirror, mirror, on the wall,
Who's the fairest of them all?

And the mirror would reply:

You are the fairest of them all.

Each year, however, Snow White grew more beautiful. One day, when the queen looked into her mirror and asked it who was the fairest of them all, the mirror replied:

You are very fair, 'tis true.
But Snow White is more fair than you!

When the queen heard that she turned green with envy.

The queen called her huntsman before her. "You are to take Snow White into the forest," she said. "Kill her there, for I do not wish to set eyes on her again. And bring me the girl's heart in this box as proof that you have done as I have ordered."

The huntsman then led Snow White deep into the forest. But as he was drawing his hunting knife to kill her, Snow White cried, "Please spare my life! Let me run away into the forest and I will never come home again!"

Snow White was so young that the huntsman took pity on her. He said to her, "Run into the woods, dear child!" Then he killed a deer and took its heart to the wicked queen as proof that Snow White was dead.

After he had gone, Snow White was alone in the forest. She was so frightened by the shapes of the trees and the rustling of the leaves that she began to run. Wild beasts sprang at her, but they did her no harm.

On she ran, over rocks and through brambles, until it began to grow dark. Snow White was so tired, she thought she could not take another step. Then up ahead she saw a tiny cottage.

Snow White went inside. Everything in the cottage was very clean and tidy—and also very small. There was a little table covered with a white cloth and set with seven little plates, each with a spoon and a knife and a cup. And against the wall, all in a row, were seven little beds.

Snow White was very hungry and thirsty. So she ate a bit of bread from each plate and drank a drop of water from each cup, for she did not want to take everything from any single one.

Then, as she was very tired, she lay down on one of the beds. Soon she was fast asleep.

A short while later, the owners of the cottage came home. They were seven dwarfs who spent their days mining in the mountains. As soon as they lit their candles the dwarfs saw that someone had been there while they were out.

"Who has been eating from my plate?" said the first.

"Who has been drinking from my cup?" cried the second.

And on it went, until the seventh dwarf caught sight of Snow White fast asleep in his bed. He called the others over, and they all stood and stared in wonder at the sleeping child.

"How beautiful she is!" they whispered, and they decided to let her go on sleeping.

The next morning, Snow White was frightened when she woke up and saw the seven dwarfs. But they smiled kindly at her and asked her her name.

"Snow White," she replied. Then she told them how her wicked stepmother had ordered the huntsman to kill her and how he had spared her her life.

"Why don't you stay here with us?" the dwarfs said. "You can cook and keep house for us, and we will take good care of you."

Snow White agreed, and so she kept the cottage for them and always had supper ready when they came home from working in the mountains.

As Snow White was alone all day, the dwarfs warned her to be careful.

"Do not let anyone in," they said, "for your wicked stepmother will surely discover where you are and come looking for you."

At that very moment the wicked queen looked into her magic mirror and asked:

Mirror, mirror, on the wall,
Who's the fairest one of all?

And the mirror replied:

You are very fair, 'tis true.
But in a cottage far away,
Where the seven dwarfs do stay,
Snow White is fairer still than you!

The wicked queen shook with rage. Snow White lived. Her magic mirror never lied. All day she schemed, until at last she settled on a plan to get rid of Snow White.

First the wicked queen made a poisoned apple. Half of it was snow-white and the other half was rosy red, and it looked delicious.

When the apple was ready, the queen disguised herself as a poor farm woman. Then she traveled to the seven dwarfs' cottage.

When the queen knocked on the door, Snow White came to the window.

"I cannot let anyone in," Snow White called out.

"But I only wish to sell you some of my apples," replied the farm woman. "Here, try one!" And she held out the poisoned apple.

But Snow White said, "No. I dare not!"

"Are you afraid I might poison you?" laughed the farm woman. "Look, I will cut the apple in two. You take the rosy red half, and I'll take the white." But Snow White did not know that the red half was poisoned.

"Very well," Snow White said, for the apple looked so delicious, she could not help herself. Eagerly, she bit into it. No sooner had she done so, than she fell down dead.

When the seven dwarfs came home that night they found Snow White lying pale and still on the ground. They called her name and tried to shake her awake, but it was no use. Snow White was truly dead.

At the palace, the wicked queen gazed into her magic mirror and asked who was the fairest of them all. The mirror replied:

You are the fairest of them all.

Finally, the wicked queen was satisfied.

The seven dwarfs wept over Snow White for three days. Then, it was time to bury her. But she looked as if she were still alive, and they could not bear to put her in the cold ground. So they made her a glass coffin and wrote her name on it in gold letters. Then they set it in the forest.

For a long time, Snow White lay in the glass coffin. Yet her beauty did not fade. One day a prince rode into the forest and saw the coffin. Snow White looked so lovely that he fell in love with her.

The prince begged the dwarfs to let him have Snow White's coffin. At last, they took pity on him and agreed.

The prince ordered his servants to carry Snow White in her glass coffin to his palace. But on the way, one of them tripped. The coffin fell, and the piece of poisoned apple flew from Snow White's throat.

Snow White opened her eyes. "Where am I?" she cried, looking up at the prince.

"You are with me," he replied, "and I wish you to marry me and stay with me forever."

The prince looked so kind and sincere that Snow White said, "Yes." And their wedding was celebrated with great joy. The seven dwarfs all came and danced and cheered.

As for the wicked queen, she was so angry that she ran into the forest and was never seen again. And with no one to wish them harm, Snow White and the prince lived happily ever after.

# The Night Before Christmas

By CLEMENT C. MOORE

Illustrated by LYNN FERRIS

'Twas the night before Christmas, when all through the house
Not a creature was stirring, not even a mouse.

The stockings were hung by the chimney with care,
In hopes that St. Nicholas soon would be there.
The children were nestled all snug in their beds,
While visions of sugarplums danced in their heads;

And Mama in her kerchief, and I in my cap,
Had just settled our brains for a long winter's nap,
When out on the lawn there arose such a clatter,
I sprang from my bed to see what was the matter.
Away to the window I flew like a flash,
Tore open the shutters and threw up the sash.
The moon on the breast of the new-fallen snow
Gave a luster of midday to objects below;

When what to my wondering eyes should appear
But a miniature sleigh and eight tiny reindeer,
With a little old driver, so lively and quick,
I knew in a moment it must be St. Nick!

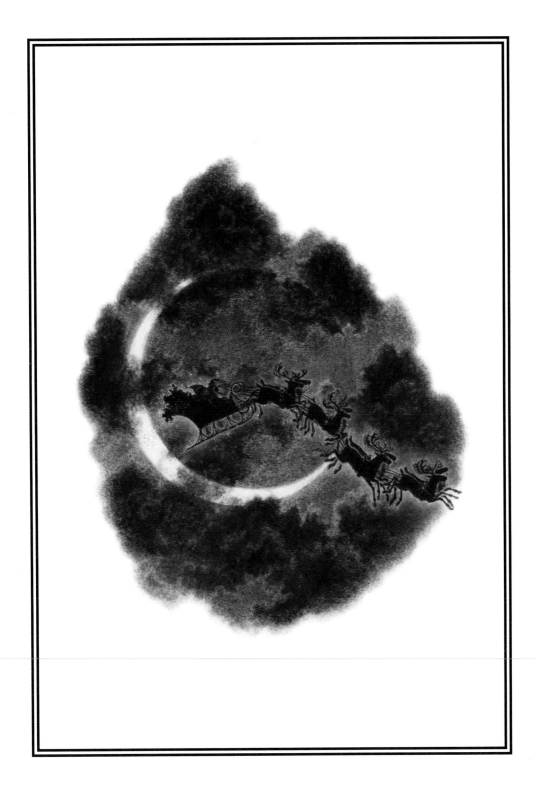

More rapid than eagles his coursers they came,
And he whistled and shouted and called them by name:
"Now, Dasher! Now, Dancer! Now, Prancer and Vixen!
On, Comet! On, Cupid! On, Donder and Blitzen!
To the top of the porch! To the top of the wall!
Now dash away! Dash away! Dash away, all!"

As dry leaves that before the wild hurricane fly,
When they meet with an obstacle, mount to the sky,
So up to the housetop the coursers they flew,
With a sleigh full of toys—and St. Nicholas too.
And then, in a twinkling, I heard on the roof
The prancing and pawing of each little hoof.
As I drew in my head and was turning around,
Down the chimney St. Nicholas came with a bound.

He was dressed all in fur, from his head to his foot,
And his clothes were all tarnished with ashes and soot;
A bundle of toys he had flung on his back,
And he looked like a peddler just opening his pack.
His eyes, how they twinkled! His dimples, how merry!
His cheeks were like roses, his nose like a cherry!
His droll little mouth was drawn up like a bow,
And the beard on his chin was as white as the snow.
The stump of a pipe he held tight in his teeth,
And the smoke, it encircled his head like a wreath.

He had a broad face and a little round belly
That shook, when he laughed, like a bowl full of jelly.
He was chubby and plump, a right jolly old elf,
And I laughed when I saw him, in spite of myself.
A wink of his eye and a twist of his head
Soon gave me to know I had nothing to dread.

He spoke not a word, but went straight to his work,
And filled all the stockings, then turned with a jerk,
And laying a finger aside of his nose,
And giving a nod, up the chimney he rose.

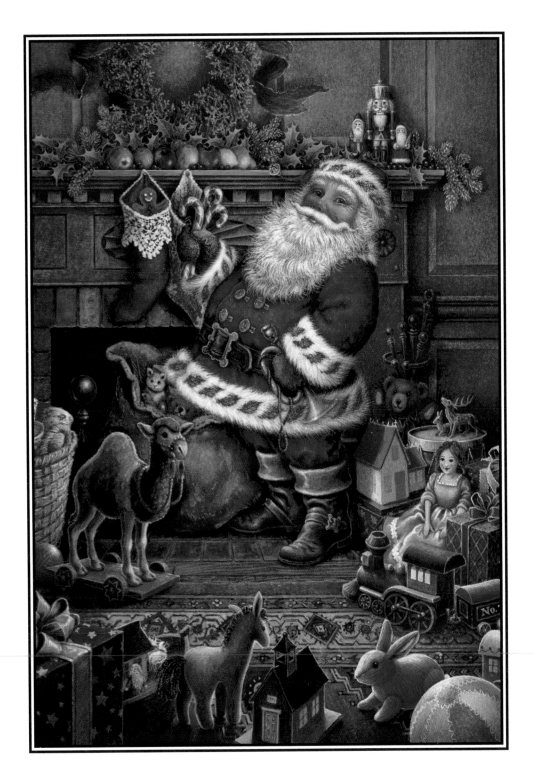

He sprang to his sleigh, to his team gave a whistle,
And away they all flew like the down of a thistle.
But I heard him exclaim, ere he drove out of sight,
"Happy Christmas to all, and to all a good night!"

# The Three Billy Goats Gruff

*Retold by* JENNIFER GREENWAY

*Illustrated by* LORETTA LUSTIG

$O$nce upon a time there were three billy goats. The name of these three goats was Gruff, so they were known as the Three Billy Goats Gruff.

The Three Billy Goats Gruff lived in a rocky field at the bottom of a grassy hill. The grass in this field was brown and tough, and the Three Billy Goats Gruff were always hungry.

The Three Billy Goats Gruff wished they could go up the hill to where the grass was green and tender. "If we could only do that," they said, "then we would all become fat and be very happy."

However, to get up the hill, the Three Billy Goats Gruff had to cross a bridge that went over a rushing stream. Under this bridge, there lived a big ugly troll who liked nothing better than to eat billy goats and anything else that crossed his path.

So the Three Billy Goats Gruff stayed where they were. But every day they looked up at the hillside and sighed, for they so longed to go there and enjoy the tender grass.

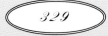

One day, the youngest Billy Goat Gruff turned to his brothers and said, "I can't bear trying to chew this tough brown grass anymore. I am going to go up the hillside to where the grass is green and sweet!"

"But what about the troll?" exclaimed the other two. "He will surely eat you up!"

"Perhaps he will," the youngest Billy Goat Gruff replied, "But if I stay in this field, I will surely starve anyway! I am going to cross that bridge."

"But you are the smallest of us all!" said the other Billy Goats Gruff. "The troll will be able to eat you with no trouble!"

"We shall see about that," said the youngest Billy Goat Gruff.

So off the youngest Billy Goat Gruff went. When he reached the bridge where the troll lived he started across it as fast as he could. *Tip-tap, tip-tap, tip-tap* went his tiny little hooves.

The big ugly troll heard something overhead, and just as the youngest Billy Goat Gruff reached the center of the bridge, the troll called out in his big voice:

"Who's that crossing my bridge?"

"It's only me," replied the youngest Billy Goat Gruff in his tiny little voice.

"Is that so?" roared the troll. "Well, I am going to eat you up!"

The youngest Billy Goat Gruff was very frightened, but he replied bravely, "Oh, please don't do that. I am so small and thin, I would hardly be enough for a snack for such a big creature as you."

"You'll do fine," the troll said.

"No," cried the youngest Billy Goat Gruff. "Wait until my brother, the second Billy Goat Gruff, comes along. He is much bigger and fatter than I. He will make you a much better supper!"

The troll was quite hungry, so he agreed to wait. The youngest Billy Goat Gruff continued on his way—*tip-tap, tip-tap, tip-tap*—up  the hillside to where the grass grew green and thick. There, the youngest Billy Goat Gruff ate to his heart's content, and he began to grow fat.

After a while, the second Billy Goat Gruff decided he would try his luck. So off he went toward the bridge where the troll lived. When he reached the bridge he started across it as fast as he could. *Trip-trap, trip-trap, trip-trap* went his middle-sized hooves. The troll heard him and cried in his big voice, "Who's that crossing my bridge?"

"It's only me," replied the second Billy Goat Gruff in his middle-sized voice.

"Is that so?" said the troll. "Well, I am going to eat you up!"

The second Billy Goat Gruff was very frightened, but he replied bravely, "Oh, no! Don't do that. I'm not nearly big and fat enough to satisfy such a big fellow like you. Wait until my brother, the third Billy Goat Gruff, comes along. He's much bigger than I, and I'm sure that he will fill you up!"

The troll, who was very hungry by now, agreed to wait once more.

So the second Billy Goat Gruff continued across the bridge—*trip-trap, trip-trap, trip-trap*—and soon he joined his younger brother on the hillside where the grass grew green and sweet.

The second Billy Goat Gruff ate and ate, and before long he was even fatter than his brother.

Now the third Billy Goat Gruff found himself all alone in the dry brown field. He decided to try his luck, too.

So off went the third Billy Goat Gruff toward the bridge where the troll lived.

When the third Billy Goat Gruff reached the bridge, he started across it as fast as he could. *TRAMP, TRAMP, TRAMP* went his big hooves. The big ugly troll heard him, and he cried out in his great big voice, "Who's that crossing my bridge?"

Then the troll poked his head up over the bridge to take a look. When the third Billy Goat Gruff saw him, he thought, "Why, that troll's not so big!" And he replied in his biggest voice, "It's only ME!"

"Is that so?" roared the troll. "Well, I'm going to eat you!"

"Let's see you try it," replied the third Billy Goat Gruff. And then he shouted:

I've got two big sharp horns
that will make you sore!
And two big pronged hooves
that will break your bones!
And lots of big sharp teeth
that will bite you all over!

Now, the troll was so hungry by this time that when he heard what the third Billy Goat said, he got mad! He jumped up onto the bridge and ran straight toward the third Billy Goat Gruff, shouting, "I'm going to eat you up right now!"

So the third Billy Goat Gruff butted the ugly troll with his big sharp horns. Then he kicked the troll with his big pronged hooves. Then he bit him all over with his big sharp teeth.

At last, the troll begged him to stop. "I promise I won't eat you!" he said. "Please, let me go!"

But the third Billy Goat Gruff kept on butting and kicking and biting him until, at last, the big ugly troll jumped off the bridge and was swept away by the rushing stream.

Then the third Billy Goat Gruff continued on his way—*TRAMP, TRAMP, TRAMP*—and soon he reached the hillside where the grass grew thick and green.

There he joined his brothers, and he ate and ate the tender grass and became very, very fat, which made him very, very happy.

So the three Billy Goats Gruff lived on the green hillside, and they all grew fatter and fatter. And for all I know they still live there today.

As for the big ugly troll, no one ever saw or heard of him again!

The text of this book was set in Goudy and the

display in Swanson by Harry Chester, Inc.,

New York City.

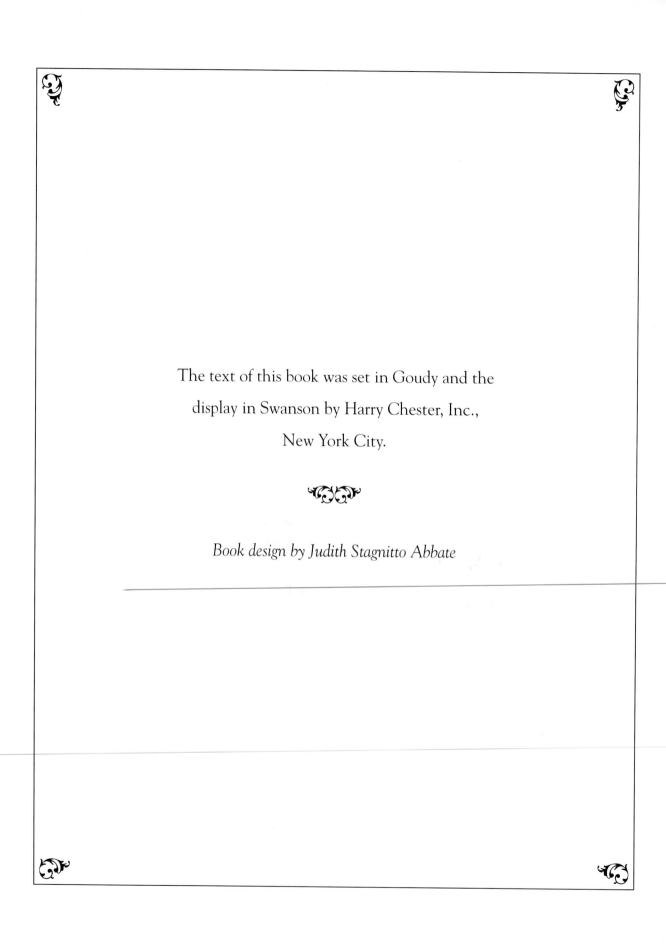

*Book design by Judith Stagnitto Abbate*